ADVENTURE TIME™

BIG ~~DOODLE~~ DUDE-L BOOK

by Kirsten Mayer
illustrated by Bob Ostrom

PSS!
PRICE STERN SLOAN
An Imprint of Penguin Group (USA) Inc.

The publisher does not have any control over and does not assume any responsibility for author or third-party websites or their content.

Published in 2013 by Price Stern Sloan, a division of Penguin Young Readers Group, 345 Hudson Street, New York, New York 10014. PSS! is a registered trademark of Penguin Group (USA) Inc. Printed in the U.S.A.

ISBN 978-0-8431-7465-6 10 9 8 7 6 5 4 3 2 1

ALWAYS LEARNING PEARSON

Makin' Bacon Pancakes

Before they do any adventuring, Finn and Jake need a snack. Jake's makin' bacon pancakes. What would you put in your pancakes?

Finn's piling his snacks into an everything burrito. What would be in your ultimate burrito?

Gettin' in Shape

Jake practices stretching into different shapes for his next quest. Help him try out some new forms by drawing them here.

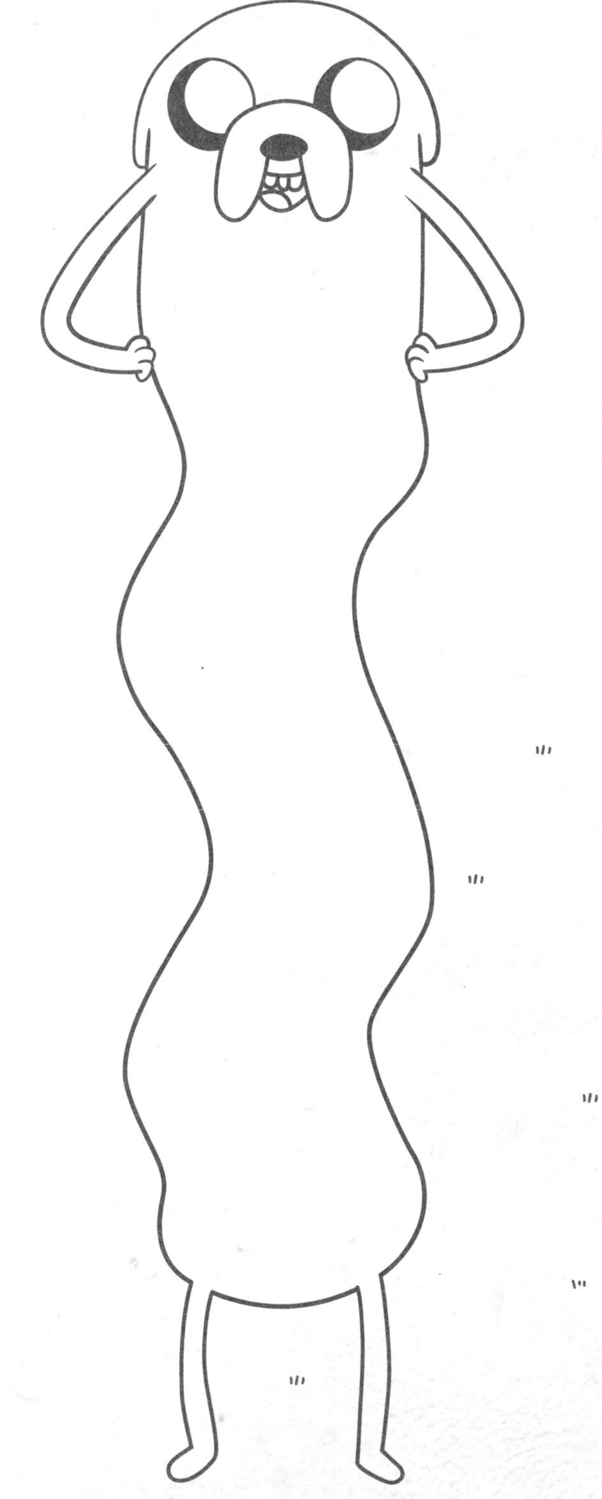

In the Tree, Part of the Tree!

Finn's throwing disc gets stuck in the tree. What else is stuck up in there?

Fight Cute!

It's a war with the Cuties! Finn and Jake feel bad for these cute little guys, so they pretend to lose a fight against them. Fill the battlefield with Cutie soldiers conquering them.

Candy Creator

Princess Bubblegum needs some new subjects in the Candy Kingdom. Draw your favorite pieces of candy and then turn them into Candy People. Give them titles, like the Mayor of Mint or Duke of Taffy.

Penguinpalooza

The Ice King needs extra help to build a new princess. Fill these pages with Gunters.

Build a Princess

If you were going to marry a princess, what would she look like? Use these ideas to build your own.

Potential ingredients:

- Pizza
- Perfume
- Logs
- Cupcakes
- Beetles

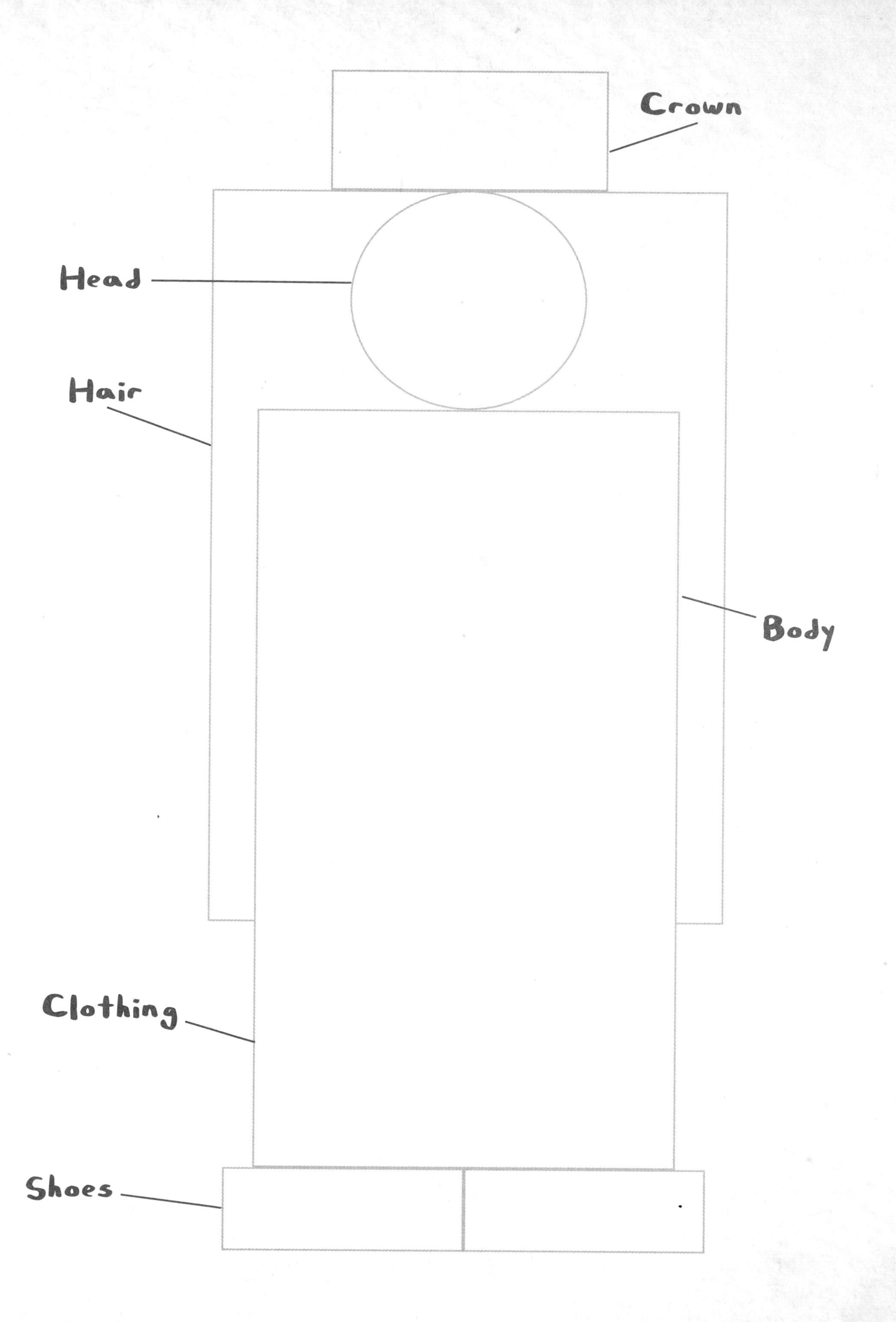

Princess ______________________________

Wizard Battle!

Which spells would you use to defeat each of these wizards in the Wizard Battle?
Winner gets a kiss from Princess Bubblegum!

BMO, PI

Something is missing, and BMO is on the case! Set up a mystery for you and your friends to solve.

What has been stolen? ______________________

List of Suspects

LSP

Chicken

Clues:

Stinky sock

Cheese

Miniverse

Finn finds a sack of mini versions of himself and his friends. Draw mini versions here of you and your friends. Write a story about what happens between them.

Once upon a time, mini me met mini ______________________ and said, Dude,

____

____

____

____

____

____

____

____

____

____

____

Songy Song Song

Practice your songwriting and write an emo tune like Marceline.
Here are some lyrics to get you started:

Daddy, why did you eat my fries?

I bought them, and they were mine.

But you ate them, yeah, you ate my fries.

And I cried, but you didn't see me cry.

Hot Time Room Machine

Prismo, Jake, and Cosmic Owl are hanging in the hot tub. While they munch pickles, you get to wish for absolutely anything you want. Draw what you would wish for.

All Aboard!

The conductor is taking everyone on a wild ride.
Draw train tracks all over Ooo.

The Look of Fear

Finn and Jake don't like the looks of the next monster they have to battle. What do you think it looks like?

Hot Stuff

Finn has a crush on Flame Princess. But after just a little peck on the cheek, she gets too happy and her flames get out of control! Fill the page with fiery hot flames!

She's Aliiiiive!

Ice King stole body parts from a few princesses to make his own monstrous wife! Help the ladies out by filling back in their missing body parts.

Ghost Fight!

The Fight King challenges you to fight his troop of ghostly gladiators.
Draw more Gladiator Ghosts here.

Rock On

Jake and his buddies form a band. Give their band a name. What instruments do they play? Draw cool rock T-shirts on everyone.

Guardians of Sunshine Level 1

Can you avoid Honey Bunny, Sleepy Sam, and Bouncy Bee to survive this video-game board?

FINISH

Lost in the Swamps!

Leave a trail of lollipops all over the swamp for Finn and Jake so they can find their way out!

FINISH

Party Animals

These bears are having a party in the belly of a giant. Fill in more bears, and don't forget to draw little pictures on their tummies.

See Food

The Jiggler doesn't eat food; he eats pictures of food! Draw some tasty treats for the Jiggler to eat.

It's Always the Cute Ones

This cute little Dimple Plant grows into a huge scary monster! Draw lots of tentacles and teeth for Finn and Marceline to fight!

PARTY

Nothing but Clouds in the Sky

Jake and Lady Rainicorn visit the Cloud Kingdom for a party. Draw the other Cloud People at the party.

Get Your Lump On

When Lumpy Space Princess bites you, you get the lumps. Draw the Lumpy version of everyone!

Finn

BMO

Jake

Lumpy Finn

Lumpy BMO

Lumpy Jake

Princess Bubblegum

Lady Rainicorn

Lumpy Princess Bubblegum

Lumpy Lady Rainicorn

Party Snacks

Finn and Jake make a bunch of snacks to munch on while watching Ice King's secret tapes. Draw some more snacks for yourself!

Dig It

Jake made a treasure map so Finn could dig up some treasure. Make a map for your friends! Don't forget to bury some treasure where X marks the spot!

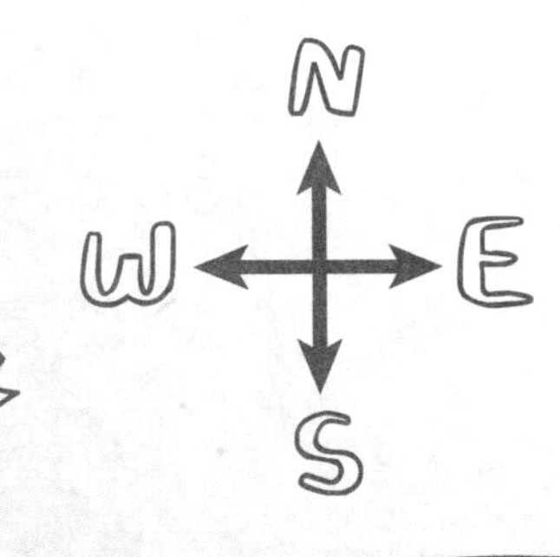

Gauntlet Garage

The Weapon Room is where Finn stores all his cool swords and stuff. Invent some other weapons for him to keep here.

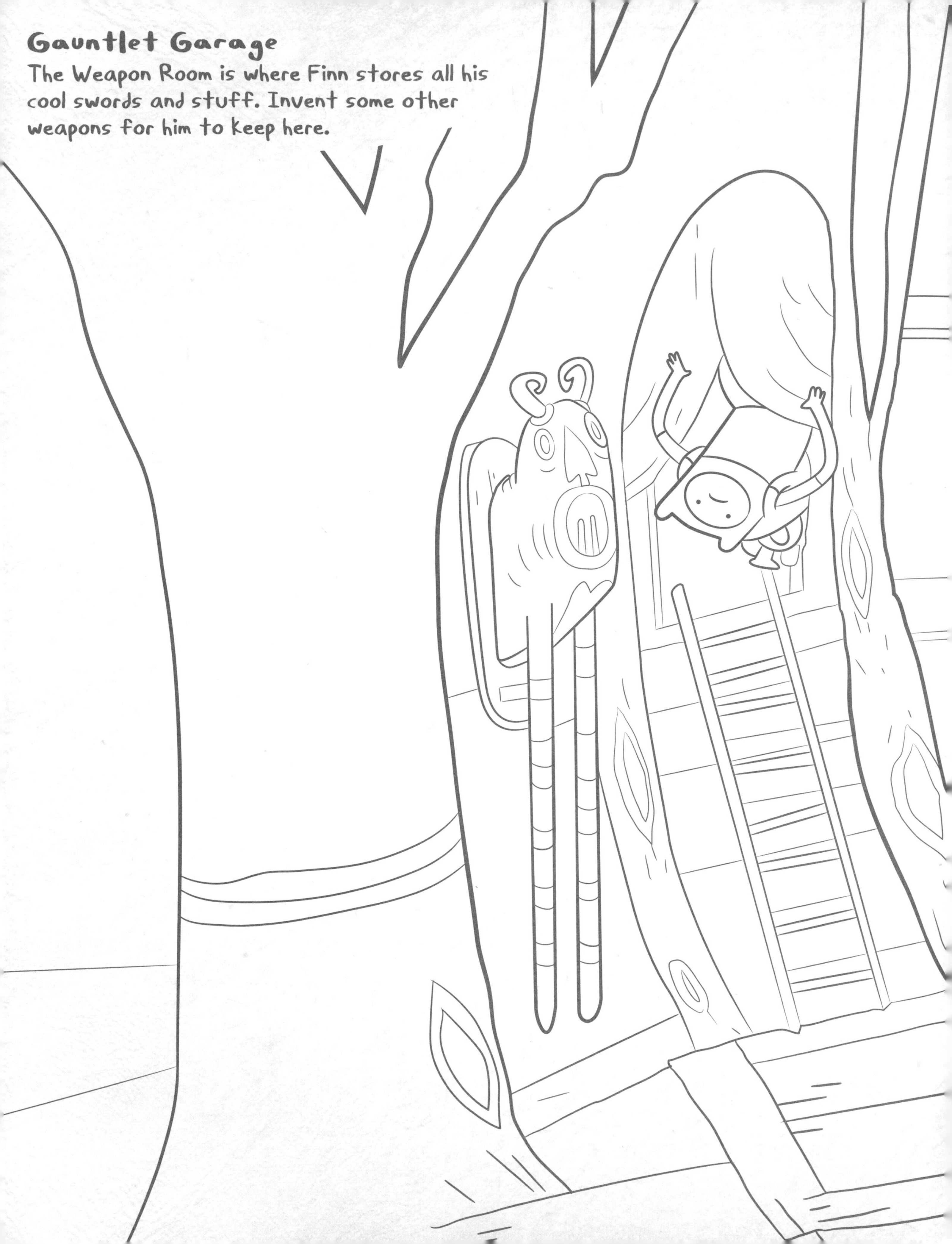

Don't Sweat(er) It

Once a year, Finn and Jake take pity on the Ice King and drink cocoa and watch movies with him. But there's one rule: Everyone has to wear a tacky sweater. Design some more sweaters here.

Night of the Living Lub Glubs

The Lub Glubs look like innocent pool toys, but they are really evil shadow creatures! Draw their true shadow forms!

How to Be a Hero

Finn found some good advice for heroes in the *Enchiridion*.

If you were writing a book for heroes, what would it look like? What would it be called? What would the chapters inside the book be about?

Spider Clan

Barb and Ed are new parents. Draw their thousands of spider babies! Fit as many of them on the page as you can!

Science Riot

Princess Bubblegum is doing another experiment. Draw the ingredients in the jars, and then draw what rises out of her slew of chemicals!

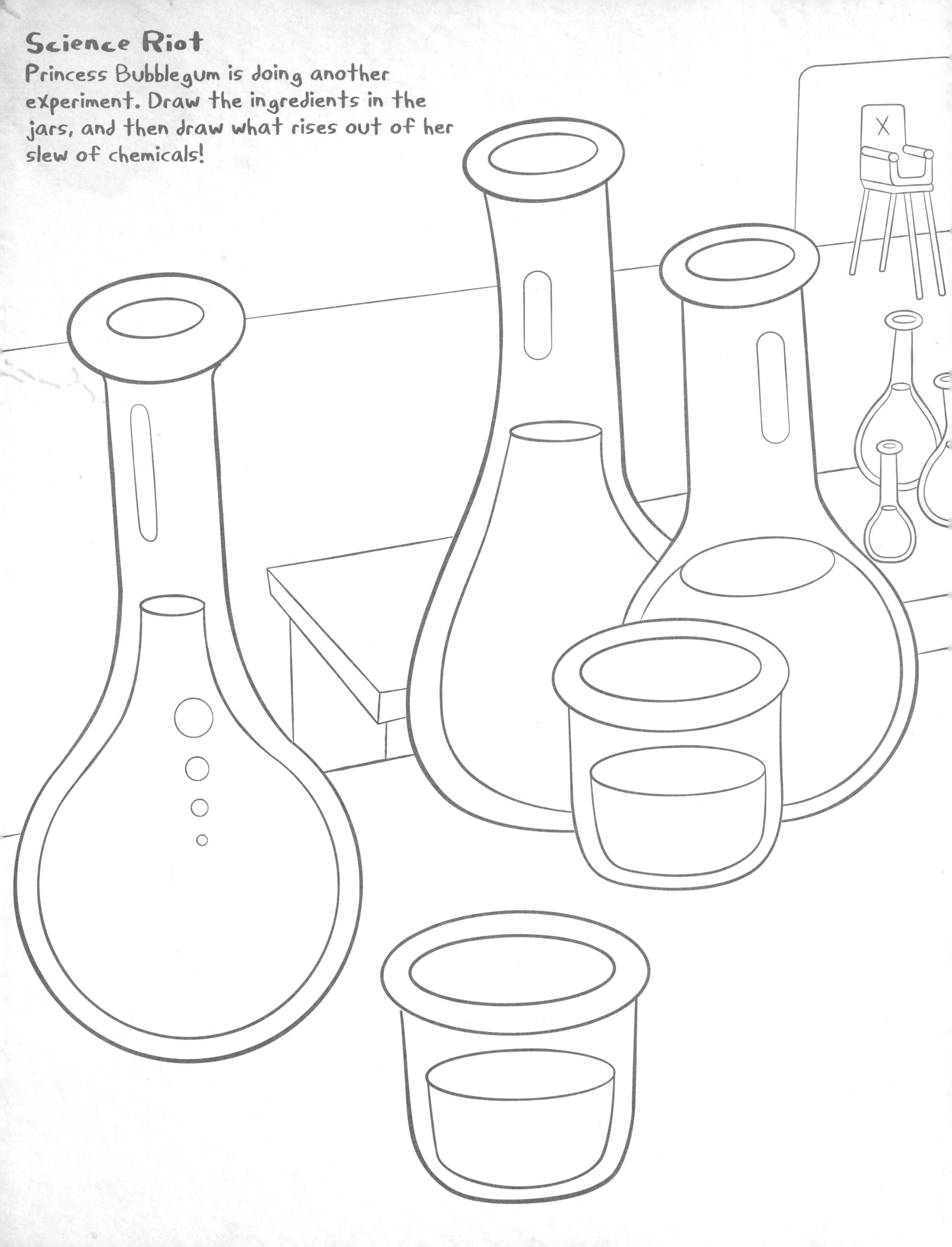

XYZ

My Lumps

LSP attracts all the boys. Dress her up in different outfits for a big date. She'll show that Brad!

Lights! Camera! Action!

Make a movie to show at Finn and Jake's movie club!
Is it a romance or a comedy?

Surprise! It's a Kitten?

Gunter laid an egg and out hatched an adorable kitten! If more Gunters hatched more eggs, what would come out?

Dream On

What if Banana Man finally made it to outer space in his rocket ship?
Who or what else would he see floating around?

A-MAZE-ING!

Find your way around the labyrinth to reach the ultimate trophy: the Ancient Psychic

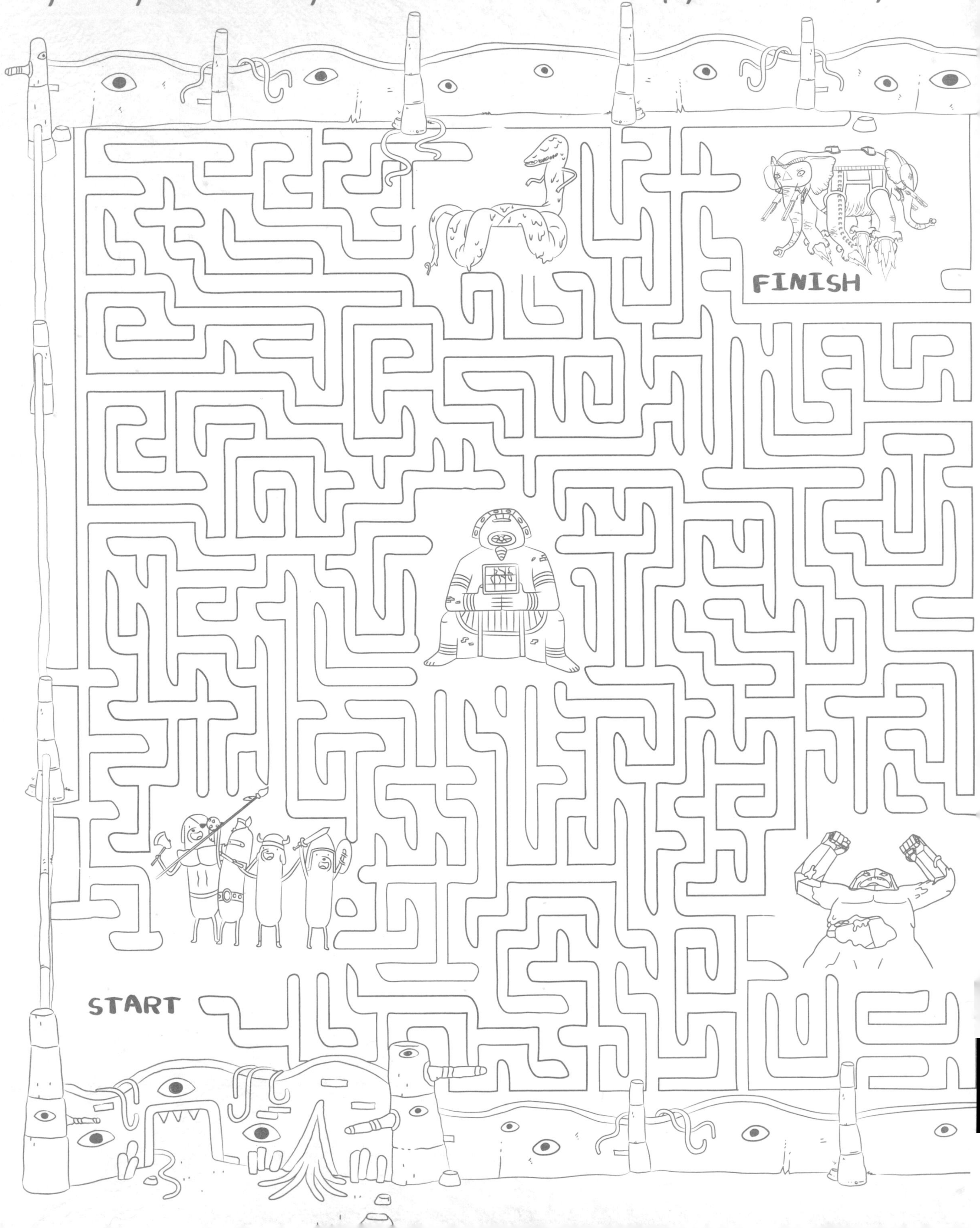

FINISH

START

Tandem War Elephant. Draw a new maze on the other page and challenge a friend.

ZOOOOOMBIIIIIEEEEES!

All the Candy People have been turned into zombies!
Draw more zombie creatures!

Deep Thoughts by LSP

Oh my glob! Did you know that it counts when your lumps are on the inside? Write some other deep thoughts here.

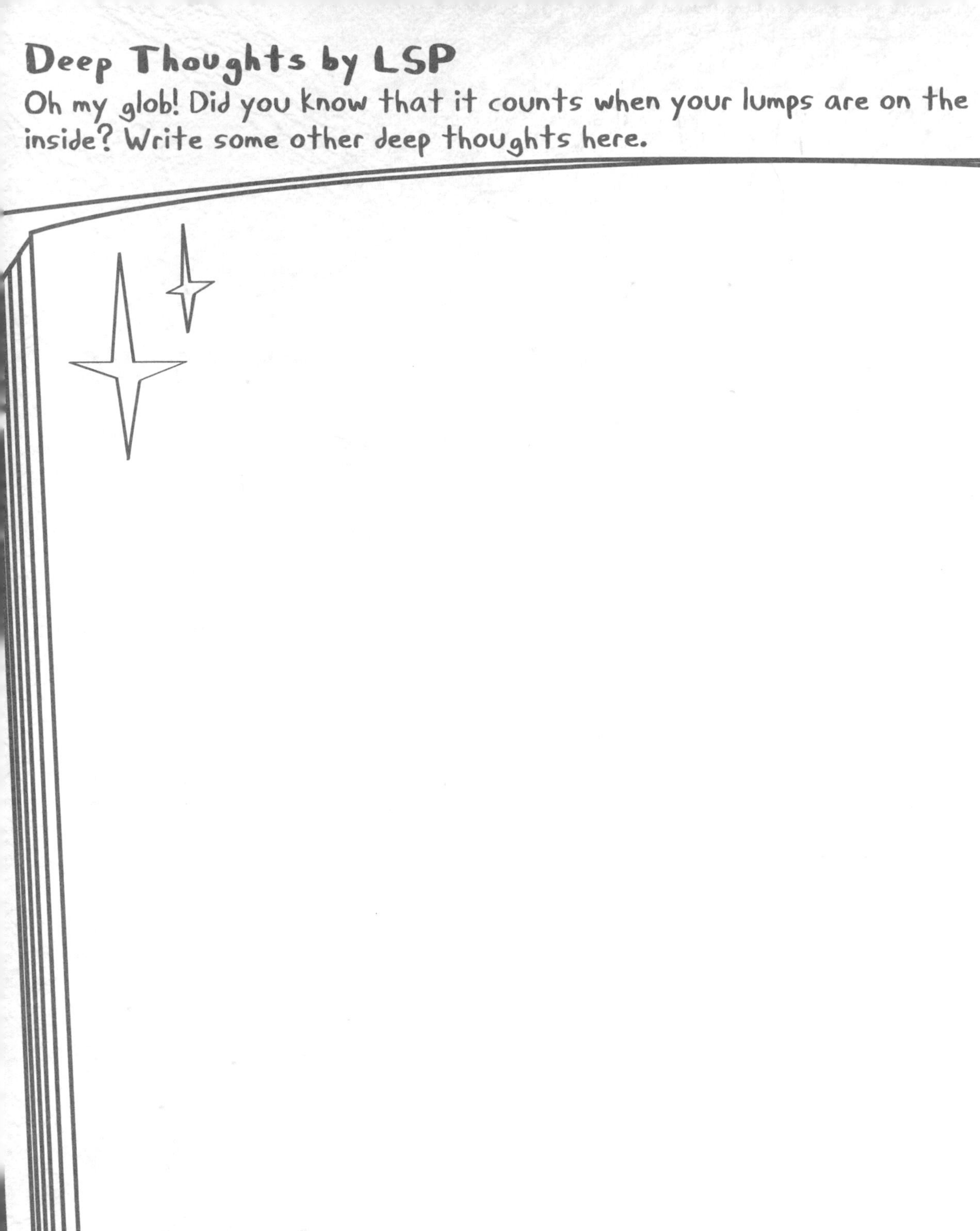

The Other Side

Fionna and Cake are fan-fiction versions of Finn and Jake. Draw the fan-fiction versions of you and your friends here.

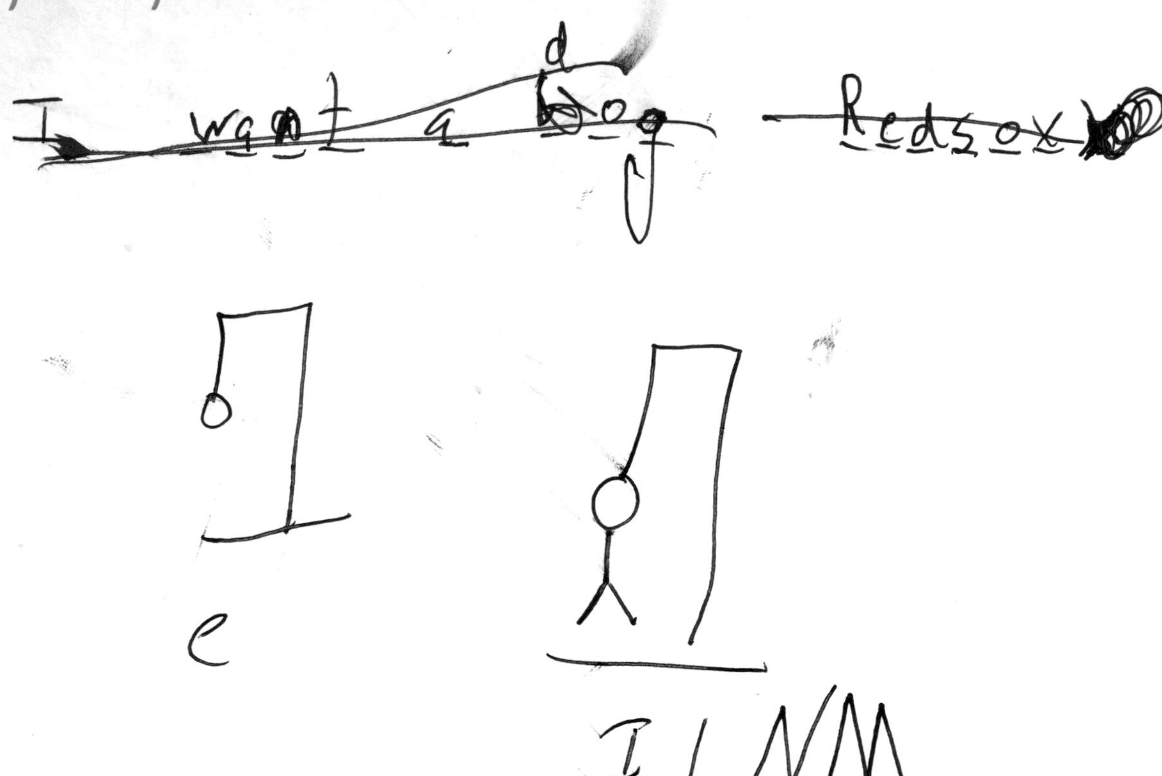

Friends Help Friends Decorate

Fionna and Cake help Prince Gumball decorate for the Biennial Gumball Ball. Draw some fun stuff around the room—like Jelly Kinders.

It's a Date?

Fionna and Cake walk through the castle gardens with Prince Gumball and Lord

Monochromicorn. Find your way through the gardens to reach Marshmallowy Mweadows.

A Gift Horse

Prince Gumball gives Fionna a pearl pygmy skull and a crystal sword hidden in a bouquet of posies. What gifts would you give your . . . chum? Draw some ideas here.

Wardrobe Change

Fionna needs a dress for the Biennial Gumball Ball! She's going as Prince Bubblegum's girlfriend. Help Cake design something fabulous, and don't forget somewhere to put her sword!

Hold on Stalactite

The Ice Queen traps Prince Gumball in ice and hangs him from the ceiling. Draw the ice crystal around him.

History Lesson

Do you know what started The Great Mushroom War?
No? Then just draw a bunch of mushrooms here.

Game On

Invent a new video game to play on BMO.

Game Name: ______________________________

Characters in the game: ______________________________

____

____

____

____

How to Win the Game: ______________________________

____

____

____

____

____

____

____

____

____

____

____

Level 1 Baddie: ______________________________

Level 2 Baddie: ______________________________

Level 3 Baddie: ______________________________

High score: ______________________________

Finn's Best Party 2nite in the Woods

Bear tries to be just like Finn—he even throws a party for all of Finn's friends and then dresses up like Finn! Finish filling in the party guests and draw Finn's clothes on the Bear—they don't fit very well!

Ice, Ice, Busy

Some businessmen are frozen in an iceberg! What else do Finn and Jake see frozen in icebergs?

Challenge Accepted

Ice-cream-eating contest! Grab a friend—one of you can be Jake, and one of you can be Finn. Set a timer for one minute, and see who can draw the most cartons of ice cream on their page! Ready, set, go!

Robot Riot

Finn built a friend named NEPTR (he ended up actually being charged by Ice King and becoming kind of evil . . . but that's a long story). Build your own robot friend!

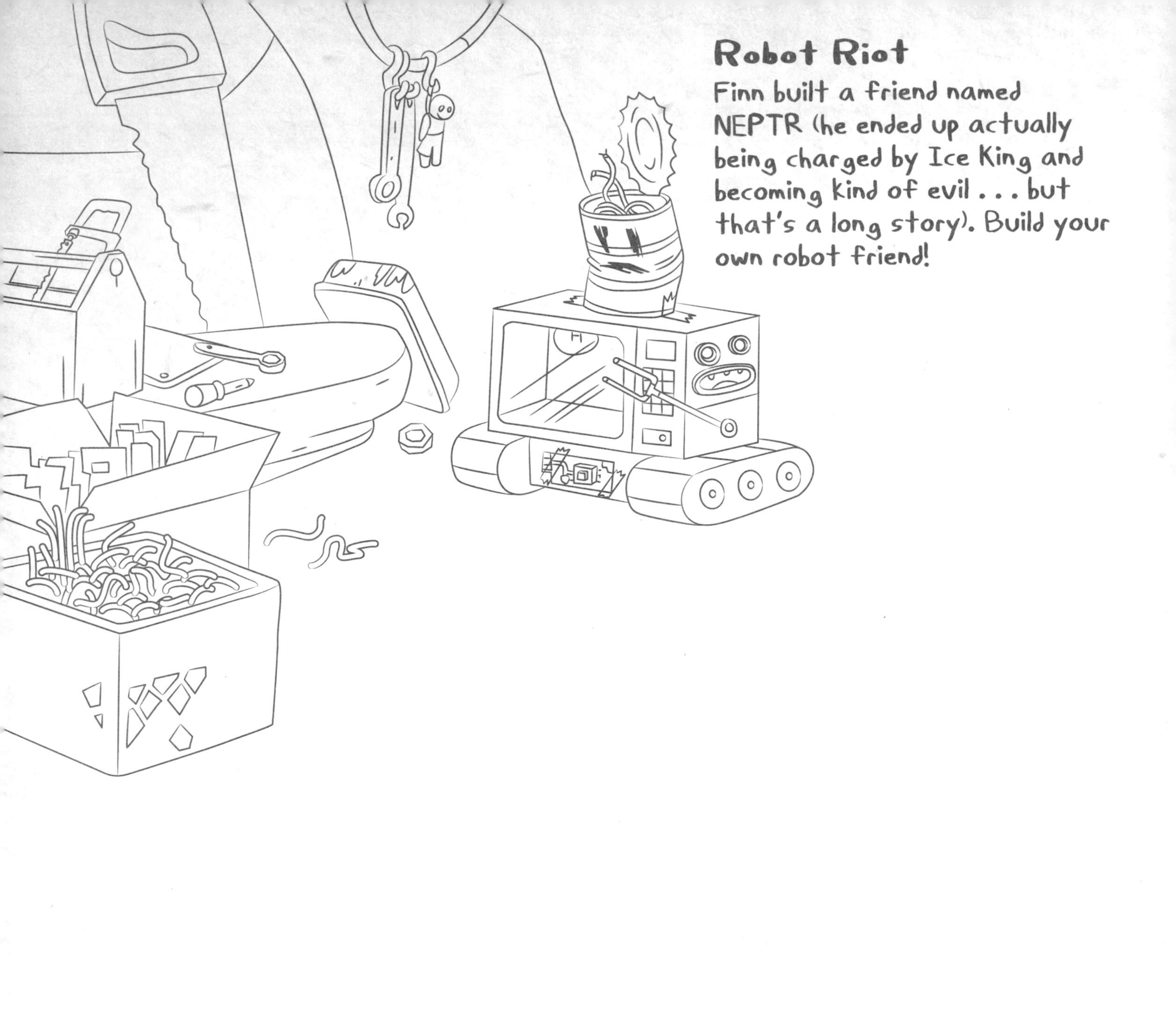

The Writing on the Zombies

Write messages on these Sign Zombies!

Imagination Zone

In his special brain space, the Ice King imagines being surrounded by princesses. Draw a ring of ladies around him.

Food Fight

Finn fights a Hamburger Monster and a Hot Dog Monster. Draw some other monsters made out of food that he can fight!

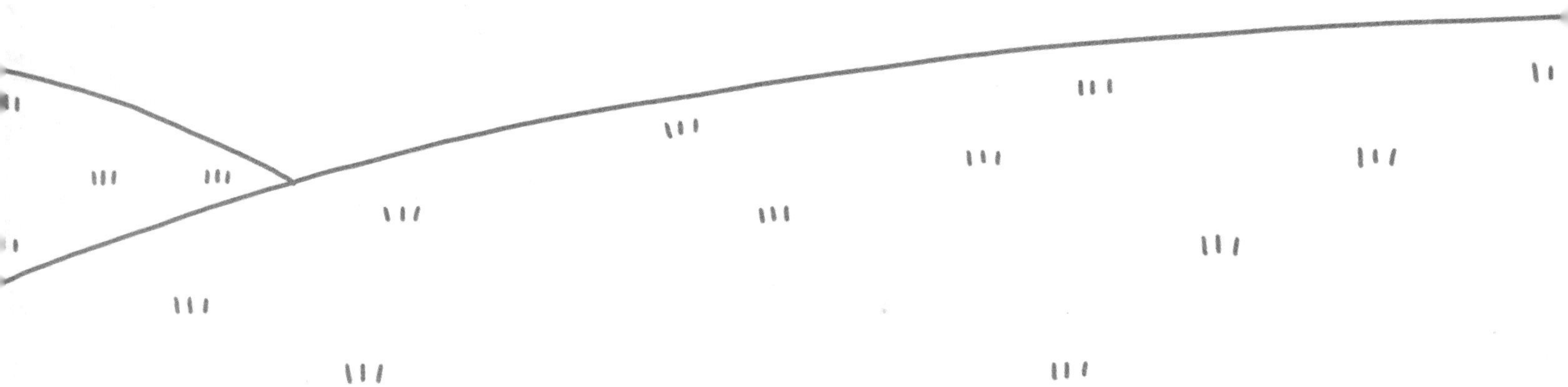

Down in the Dump

What can you find in the River of Junk—other than Gary the Mermaid Queen? Draw in some interesting junk!

Dinner in Disguise

The pals are attending a murder-mystery dinner. Draw costumes for everyone and give them names for the characters they are "playing" for dinner!

Meow Mix

Finn breaks open a bottle of Caturday Surprise. Ghost cats run everywhere! Fill these pages with more cats.

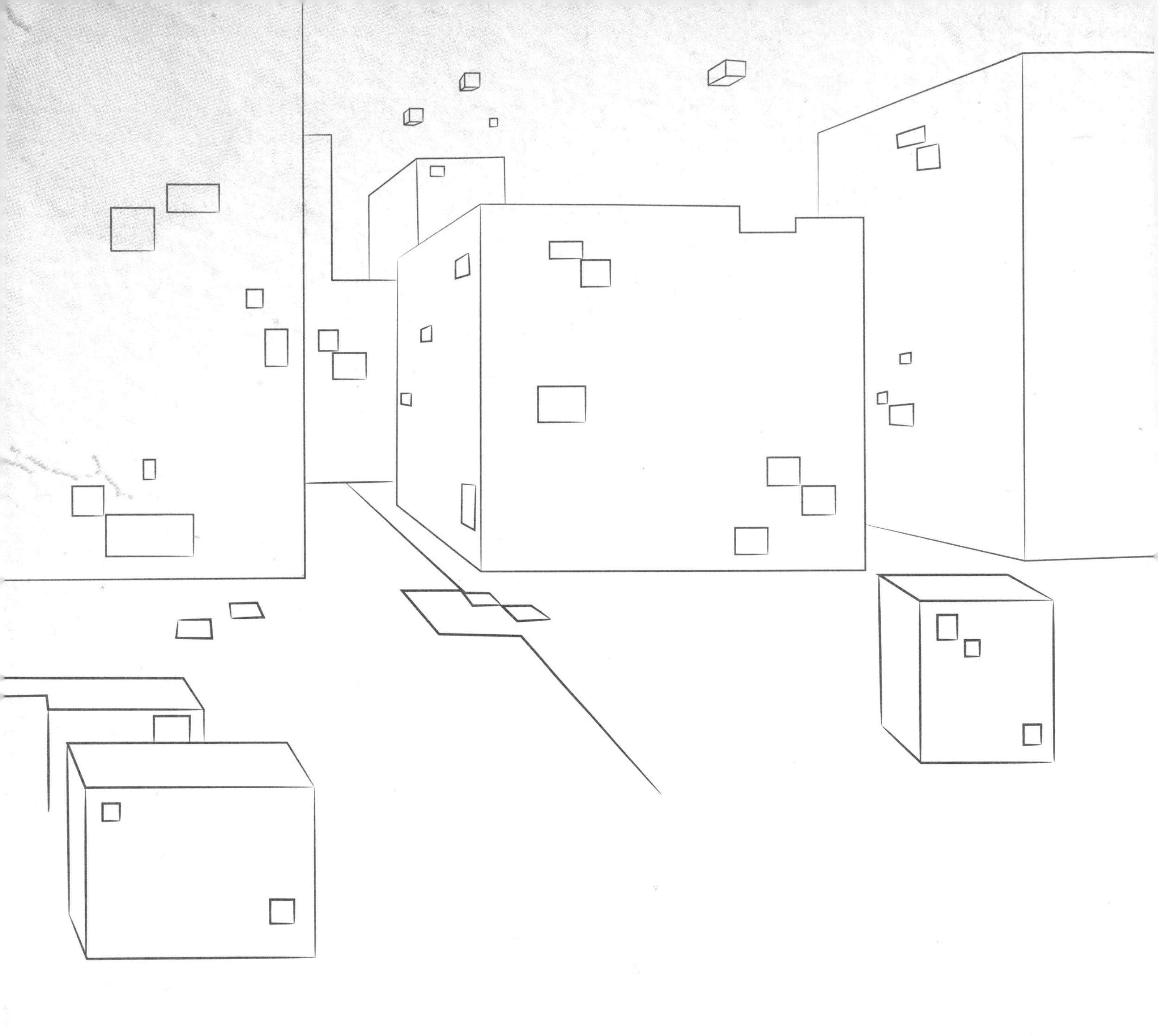

It's Hip To Be Square

Finn and Jake visit Cube Village. Fill the page with more cubical buildings.

One is the Loneliest Lemon

The Earl of Lemongrab is crabby because he's alone.
Create some Lemongrab clones to keep him company.

Heart Less

Draw Ricardio a bigger body with stolen body parts!

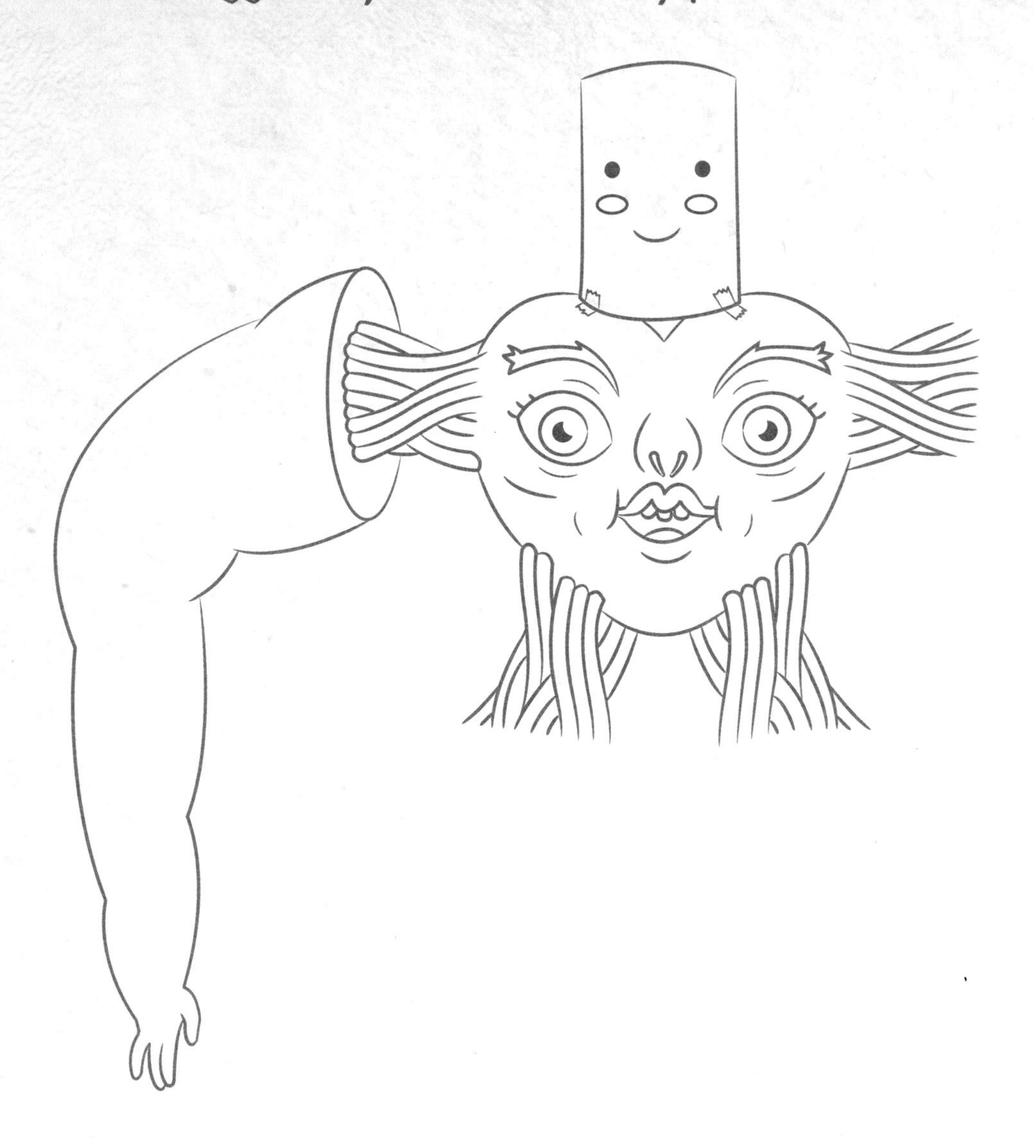

Out-of-Body Experience

Ricardio is the Ice King's heart. If one of your body parts were going to run around on its own, which would it be? Draw it here and give it a name.

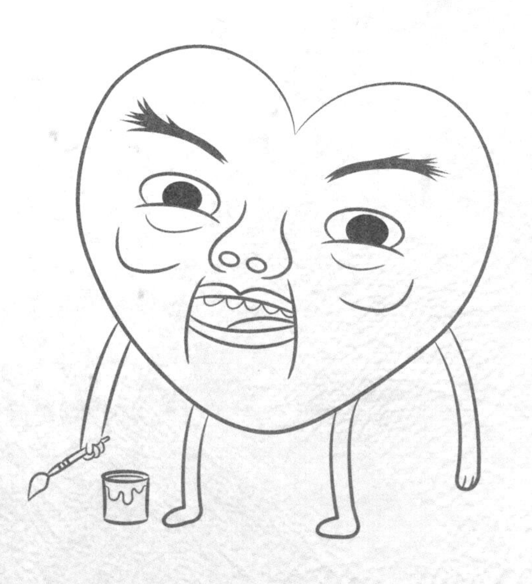

Party On

The Party God grants one wish—draw what you would wish for here!

Winter Wonderland

Finn and Jake hang out with the Snow Golem. Draw some of their friends sledding or making snow angels, and add some snowmen, too!

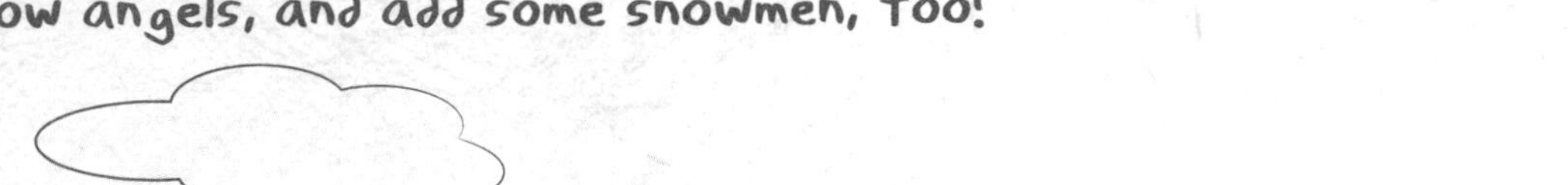

Picture Perfect

Princess Bubblegum has a lot of portraits hanging in the sitting room of Candy Castle. Most of them are of her—but some other people made it onto the wall, too. Draw portraits in the frames of PB's favorite people.

Ghost-Ship Vortex

Finn and Jake have to rescue Slime Princess! Draw more shipwrecks in the vortex for them to swim past.

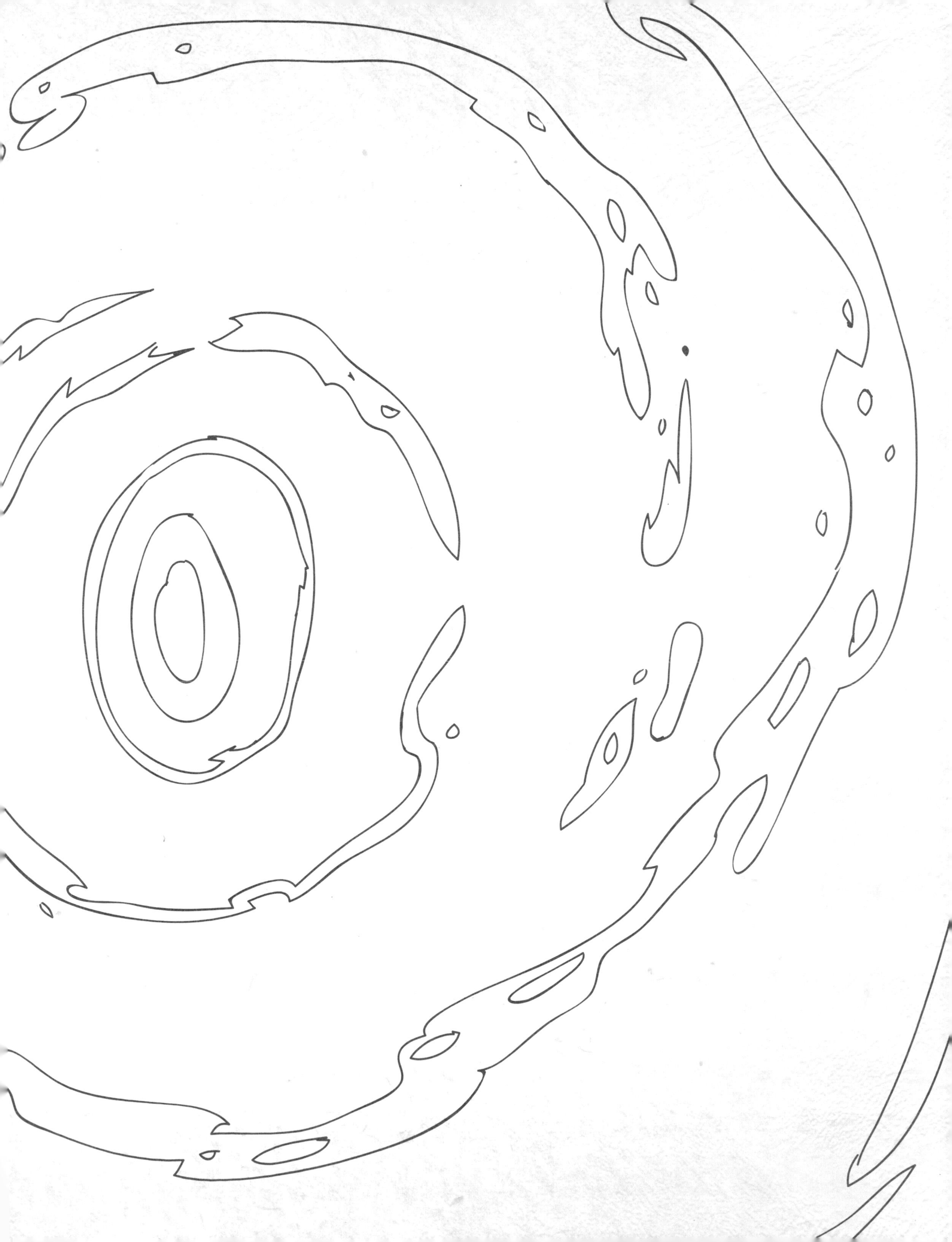

Hats On

Finn feels weird without his hat on. What would everyone else look like if they wore a hat like his? Draw one on everybody below to see!

Suit Up

BMO likes to play soccer and learn fighting. Draw some more outfits for other sports BMO might want to try.